The Hyborian Age

by

Robert E. Howard

(Nothing in this article is to be considered as an attempt to advance any theory in opposition to accepted history. It is simply a fictional background for a series of fiction-stories. When I began writing the Conan stories a few years ago, I prepared this 'history' of his age and the peoples of that age, in order to lend him and his sagas a greater aspect of realness. And I found that by adhering to the 'facts' and spirit of that history, in writing the stories, it was easier to visualize (and therefore to present) him as a real flesh-and-blood character rather than a ready-made product. In writing about him and his adventures in the various kingdoms of his Age, I have never violated the 'facts' or spirit of the 'history' here set

1

down, but have followed the lines of that history as closely as the writer of actual historical-fiction follows the lines of actual history. I have used this 'history' as a guide in all the stories in this series that I have written.)

Of that epoch known by the Nemedian chroniclers as the Pre-Cataclysmic Age, little is known except the latter part, and that is veiled in the mists of legendry. Known history begins with the waning of the Pre-Cataclysmic civilization, dominated by the kingdoms of Kamelia, Valusia, Verulia, Grondar, Thule and Commoria. These peoples spoke a similar language, arguing a common origin. There were other kingdoms, equally civilized, but inhabited by different, and apparently older races.

The barbarians of that age were the Picts, who lived on islands far out on the western ocean; the Atlanteans, who dwelt on a small continent between the Pictish Islands and the main, or Thurian Continent; and the Lemurians, who inhabited a chain of large islands in the eastern hemisphere.

There were vast regions of unexplored land. The civilized kingdoms, though enormous in extent, occupied a comparatively small portion of the whole planet. Valusia was the western-most kingdom of the Thurian Continent; Grondar the eastern-most. East of Grondar, whose people were less highly cultured than those of their kindred kingdoms, stretched a wild and barren expanse of deserts. Among the less arid stretches of desert, in the jungles, and among the mountains, lived scattered clans and tribes of primitive savages. Far to the south there was a mysterious civilization, unconnected with the Thurian culture, and apparently pre-human in its nature. On the far-eastern shores of the Continent there lived another race, human, but mysterious and non-Thurian, with which the Lemurians from time to time came in contact. They apparently came from a shadowy and nameless continent lying somewhere east of the Lemurian Islands.

The Thurian civilization was crumbling; their armies were composed largely of barbarian mercenaries. Picts, Atlanteans and Lemurians were their generals, their statesmen, often their kings. Of the bickerings of the kingdoms, and the wars between Valusia and Commoria, as well as the conquests by which the Atlanteans founded a kingdom on the mainland, there were more legends than accurate history.

Then the Cataclysm rocked the world. Atlantis and Lemuria sank, and the Pictish Islands were heaved up to form the mountain peaks of a new continent. Sections of the Thurian Continent vanished under the waves, or sinking, formed great inland lakes and seas. Volcanoes broke forth and terrific earthquakes shook down the shining cities of the empires. Whole nations were blotted out.

The barbarians fared a little better than the civilized races. The inhabitants of the Pictish Islands were destroyed, but a great colony of them, settled among the mountains of Valusia's southern frontier to serve as a buffer against foreign invasion, was untouched. The Continental kingdom of the Atlanteans likewise escaped the common ruin, and to it came thousands of their tribesmen in ships from the sinking land. Many Lemurians escaped to the eastern coast of the Thurian Continent, which was comparatively untouched. There they were enslaved by the ancient race which already dwelt there, and their history, for thousands of years, is a history of brutal servitude.

In the western part of the Continent, changing conditions created strange forms of plant and animal life. Thick jungles covered the plains, great rivers cut their roads to the sea, wild mountains were heaved up, and lakes covered the ruins of old cities in fertile valleys. To the Continental kingdom of the Atlanteans, from sunken areas, swarmed myriads of beasts and savages—ape-men and apes. Forced to battle continually for their lives, they yet managed to retain vestiges of their former state of highly advanced barbarism. Robbed of metals and ores, they became workers in stone like their distant ancestors, and had attained a real artistic level, when their struggling culture came into contact with the powerful Pictish nation. The Picts had also reverted to flint, but had advanced more rapidly in the matter of population and war-science. They had none of the Atlanteans' artistic nature; they were a ruder, more practical, more prolific race. They left no pictures painted or carved on ivory, as did their enemies, but they left remarkably efficient flint weapons in plenty.

These stone-age kingdoms clashed, and in a series of bloody wars, the outnumbered Atlanteans were hurled back into a state of savagery, and the evolution of the Picts was halted. Five hundred years after the Cataclysm the barbaric kingdoms have vanished. It is now a nation of savages—the Picts—carrying on continual warfare with tribes of savages—the Atlanteans. The Picts had the advantage of numbers and unity, whereas the Atlanteans had fallen into loosely knit clans. That was the west of that day.

In the distant east, cut off from the rest of the world by the heaving up of gigantic mountains and the forming of a chain of vast lakes, the Lemurians are toiling as slaves of their ancient masters. The far south is still veiled in mystery. Untouched by the Cataclysm, its destiny is still pre-human. Of the civilized races of the Thurian Continent, a remnant of one of the non-Valusian nations dwells among the low mountains of the southeast—the Zhemri. Here and there about the world are scattered clans of apish savages, entirely ignorant of the rise and fall of the great civilizations. But in the far north another people are slowly coming into existence.

At the time of the Cataclysm, a band of savages, whose development was not much above that of the Neanderthal, fled to the north to escape destruction. They found the snow-countries inhabited only by a species of ferocious snow-apes—huge shaggy white animals, apparently native to that climate. These they fought and drove beyond the Arctic circle, to perish, as the savages thought. The latter, then, adapted themselves to their hardy new environment and throve.

After the Pictish-Atlantean wars had destroyed the beginnings of what might have been a new culture, another, lesser cataclysm further altered the appearance of the original continent, left a great inland sea where the chain of lakes had been, to further separate west from east, and the attendant earthquakes, floods and volcanoes completed the ruin of the barbarians which their tribal wars had begun.

A thousand years after the lesser cataclysm, the western world is seen to be a wild country of jungles and lakes and torrential rivers. Among the forest-covered hills of the northwest exist wandering bands of ape-men, without human speech, or the knowledge of fire or the use of implements. They are the descendants of the Atlanteans, sunk back into the squalling chaos of jungle-bestiality from which ages ago their ancestors so laboriously crawled. To the southwest dwell scattered clans of degraded, cave-dwelling savages, whose speech is of the most primitive form, yet who still retain the name of Picts, which has come to mean merely a term designating men—themselves, to distinguish them from the true beasts with which they contend for life and food. It is their only link with their former stage. Neither the squalid Picts nor the apish Atlanteans have any contact with other tribes or peoples.

Far to the east, the Lemurians, levelled almost to a bestial plane themselves by the brutishness of their slavery, have risen and destroyed their masters. They are savages stalking among the ruins of a strange civilization. The survivors of that civilization, who have escaped the fury of their slaves, have come westward. They fall upon that mysterious pre-human kingdom of the south and overthrow it, substituting their own culture, modified by contact with the older one. The newer kingdom is called Stygia, and remnants of the older nation seemed to have survived, and even been worshipped, after the race as a whole had been destroyed.

Here and there in the world small groups of savages are showing signs of an upward trend; these are scattered and unclassified. But in the north, the tribes are growing. These people are called Hyborians, or Hybori; their god was Bori—some great chief, whom legend made even more ancient as the king who led them into the north, in the days of the great Cataclysm, which the tribes remember only in distorted folklore.

They have spread over the north, and are pushing southward in leisurely treks. So far they have not come in contact with any other races; their wars have been with one another. Fifteen hundred years in the north country have made them a tall, tawny-haired, grey-eyed race, vigorous and warlike, and already exhibiting a well-defined artistry and poetism of nature. They still live mostly by the hunt, but the southern tribes have been raising cattle for some centuries. There is one exception in their so far complete isolation from other races: a wanderer into the far north returned with the news that the supposedly deserted ice wastes were inhabited by an extensive tribe of ape-like men, descended, he swore, from the beasts driven out of the more habitable land by the ancestors of the Hyborians. He urged that a large war-party be sent beyond the arctic circle to exterminate these beasts, whom he swore were evolving into true men. He was jeered at; a small band of adventurous young warriors followed him into the north, but none returned.

But tribes of the Hyborians were drifting south, and as the population increased this movement became extensive. The following age was an epoch of wandering and conquest. Across the history of the world tribes and drifts of tribes move and shift in an everchanging panorama.

Look at the world five hundred years later. Tribes of tawny-haired Hyborians have moved southward and westward, conquering and destroying many of the small unclassified clans. Absorbing the blood of conquered races, already the descendants of the older drifts have begun to show modified racial traits, and these mixed races are attacked fiercely by new, purer-blooded drifts, and swept before them, as a broom sweeps debris impartially, to become even more mixed and mingled in the tangled debris of races and tag-ends of races.

As yet the conquerors have not come in contact with the older races. To the southeast the descendants of the Zhemri, given impetus by new blood resulting from admixture with some unclassified tribe, are beginning to seek to revive some faint shadow of their ancient culture. To the west the apish Atlanteans are beginning the long climb upward. They have completed the cycle of existence; they have long forgotten their former existence as men; unaware of any other former state, they are starting the climb unhelped and unhindered by human memories. To the south of them the Picts remain savages, apparently defying the laws of Nature by neither progressing nor retrogressing. Far to the south dreams the ancient mysterious kingdom of Stygia. On its eastern borders wander clans of nomadic savages, already known as the Sons of Shem.

Next to the Picts, in the broad valley of Zingg, protected by great mountains, a nameless band of primitives, tentatively classified as akin to the Shemites, has evolved an advanced agricultural system and existence.

Another factor has added to the impetus of Hyborian drift. A tribe of that race has discovered the use of stone in building, and the first Hyborian kingdom has come into being—the rude and barbaric kingdom of Hyperborea, which had its beginning in a crude fortress of boulders heaped to repel tribal attack. The people of this tribe soon abandoned their horse-hide tents for stone houses, crudely but mightily built, and thus protected, they grew strong. There are few more dramatic events in history than the rise of the rude, fierce kingdom of Hyperborea, whose people turned abruptly from their nomadic life to rear dwellings of naked stone, surrounded by cyclopean walls—a race scarcely emerged from the polished stone age, who had by a freak of chance, learned the first rude principles of architecture.

The rise of this kingdom drove forth many other tribes, for, defeated in the war, or refusing to become tributary to their castle-dwelling kinsmen, many clans set forth on long treks that took them halfway around the world. And already the more northern tribes are beginning to be harried by gigantic blond savages, not much more advanced than ape-men.

The tale of the next thousand years is the tale of the rise of the Hyborians, whose warlike tribes dominate the western world. Rude kingdoms are taking shape. The tawny-haired invaders have encountered the Picts, driving them into the barren lands of the west. To the northwest, the descendants of the Atlanteans, climbing unaided from apedom into primitive savagery, have not yet met the conquerors. Far to the east the Lemurians are evolving a strange semi-civilization of their own. To the south the Hyborians have founded the kingdom of Koth, on the borders of those pastoral countries known as the Lands of Shem, and the savages of those lands, partly through contact with the Hyborians, partly through contact with the Stygians who have ravaged them for centuries, are emerging from barbarism. The blond savages of the far north have grown in power and numbers so that the northern Hyborian tribes move southward, driving their kindred clans before them. The ancient kingdom of Hyperborea is overthrown by one of these northern tribes, which, however, retains the old name. Southeast of Hyperborea a kingdom of the Zhemri has come into being, under the name of Zamora. To the southwest, a tribe of Picts have invaded the fertile valley of Zingg, conquered the agricultural people there, and settled among them. This mixed race was in turn conquered later by a roving tribe of Hybori, and from these mingled elements came the kingdom of Zingara.

Five hundred years later the kingdoms of the world are clearly defined. The kingdoms of the Hyborians—Aquilonia, Nemedia, Brythunia, Hyperborea, Koth, Ophir, Argos, Corinthia, and one known as the Border Kingdom—dominate the western world. Zamora lies to the east, and Zingara to the southwest of these kingdoms—people alike in darkness of complexion and exotic habits, but otherwise unrelated. Far to the south sleeps Stygia, untouched by foreign invasion, but the peoples of Shem have exchanged the Stygian yoke for the less galling one of Koth. The dusky masters have been driven south of the great river Styx, Nilus, or Nile, which, flowing north from the shadowy hinterlands, turns almost at right angles and flows almost due west through the pastoral meadowlands of Shem, to empty into the great sea. North of Aquilonia, the western-most Hyborian kingdom, are the Cimmerians, ferocious savages, untamed by the invaders, but advancing rapidly because of contact with them; they are the descendants of the Atlanteans, now progressing more steadily than their old enemies the Picts, who dwell in the wilderness west of Aquilonia.

Another five centuries and the Hybori peoples are the possessors of a civilization so virile that contact with it virtually snatched out of the wallow of savagery such tribes as it touched. The most powerful kingdom is Aquilonia, but others vie with it in strength and mixed race; the nearest to the ancient root-stock are the Gundermen of Gunderland, a northern province of Aquilonia. But this mixing has not weakened the race. They are supreme in the western world, though the barbarians of the wastelands are growing in strength.

In the north, golden-haired, blue-eyed barbarians, descendants of the blond arctic savages, have driven the remaining Hyborian tribes out of the snow countries, except the ancient kingdom of Hyperborea, which resists their onslaught. Their country is called Nordheim, and they are divided into the red-haired Vanir of Vanaheim, and the yellow-haired Æsir of Asgard.

Now the Lemurians enter history again as Hyrkanians. Through the centuries they have pushed steadily westward, and now a tribe skirts the southern end of the great inland sea—Vilayet—and establishes the kingdom of Turan on the southwestern shore. Between the inland sea and the eastern borders of the native kingdoms lie vast expanses of steppes and in the extreme north and extreme south, deserts. The non-Hyrkanian dwellers of these territories are scattered and pastoral, unclassified in the north, Shemitish in the south, aboriginal, with a thin strain of Hyborian blood from wandering conquerors. Toward the latter part of the period other Hyrkanian clans push westward, around the northern extremity of the inland sea, and clash with the eastern outposts of the Hyperboreans.

Glance briefly at the peoples of that age. The dominant of Hyborians are no longer uniformly tawny-haired and grey-eyed. They have mixed with other races. There is a strong Shemitish, even a Stygian strain among the peoples of Koth, and to a lesser extent, of Argos, while in the case of the latter, admixture with the Zingarans has been more extensive than with the Shemites. The eastern Brythunians have intermarried with the dark-skinned Zamorians, and the people of southern Aquilonia have mixed with the brown Zingarans until black hair and brown eyes are the dominant type in Poitain, the southern-most province. The ancient kingdom of Hyperborea is more aloof than the others, yet there is alien blood in plenty in its veins, from the capture of foreign women—Hyrkanians, Æsir and Zamorians. Only in the province of Gunderland, where the people keep no slaves, is the pure Hyborian stock found unblemished. But the barbarians have kept their bloodstream pure; the Cimmerians are tall and powerful, with dark hair and blue or grey eyes. The people of Nordheim are of similar build, but with white skins, blue eyes and golden or red hair. The Picts are of the same type as they always were—short, very dark, with black eyes and hair. The Hyrkanians are dark and generally tall and slender, though a squat slant-eyed type is more and more common among them, resulting from mixture with a curious race of intelligent, though stunted, aborigines, conquered by them among the mountains east of Vilayet, on their westward drift. The Shemites are generally of medium height, though sometimes when mixed with Stygian blood, gigantic, broadly and strongly built, with hook noses, dark eyes and blue-black hair. The Stygians are tall and well made, dusky, straight-featured—at least the ruling classes are of that type. The lower classes are a down-trodden, mongrel horde, a mixture of negroid, Stygian, Shemitish, even Hyborian bloods. South of Stygia are the vast black kingdoms of the Amazons, the Kushites, the Atlaians and the hybrid empire of Zembabwe.

Between Aquilonia and the Pictish wilderness lie the Bossonian marches, peopled by descendants of an aboriginal race, conquered by a tribe of Hyborians, early in the first ages of the Hyborian drift. This mixed people never attained the civilization of the purer Hyborians, and was pushed by them to the very fringe of the civilized world. The Bossonians are of medium height and complexion, their eyes brown or grey, and they are mesocephalic. They live mainly by agriculture, in large walled villages, and are part of the Aquilonian kingdom. Their marches extend from the Border Kingdom in the north to

Zingara in the southwest, forming a bulwark for Aquilonia against both the Cimmerians and the Picts. They are stubborn defensive fighters, and centuries of warfare against northern and western barbarians have caused them to evolve a type of defense almost impregnable against direct attack.

Five hundred years later the Hyborian civilization was swept away. Its fall was unique in that it was not brought about by internal decay, but by the growing power of the barbarian nations and the Hyrkanians. The Hyborian peoples were overthrown while their vigorous culture was in its prime.

Yet it was Aquilonia's greed which brought about that overthrow, though indirectly. Wishing to extend their empire, her kings made war on their neighbors. Zingara, Argos and Ophir were annexed outright, with the western cities of Shem, which had, with their more eastern kindred, recently thrown off the yoke of Koth. Koth itself, with Corinthia and the eastern Shemitish tribes, was forced to pay

Aquilonia tribute and lend aid in wars. An ancient feud had existed between Aquilonia and Hyperborea, and the latter now marched to meet the armies of her western rival. The plains of the Border Kingdom were the scene of a great and savage battle, in which the northern hosts were utterly defeated, and retreated into their snowy fastnesses, whither the victorious Aquilonians did not pursue them. Nemedia, which had successfully resisted the western kingdom for centuries, now drew Brythunia and Zamora, and secretly, Koth, into an alliance which bade fair to crush the rising empire. But before their armies could join battle, a new enemy appeared in the east, as the Hyrkanians made their first real thrust at the western world. Reinforced by adventurers from east of Vilayet, the riders of Turan swept over Zamora, devastated eastern Corinthia, and were met on the plains of Brythunia by the Aquilonians who defeated them and hurled them flying eastward. But the back of the alliance was broken, and

Nemedia took the defensive in future wars, aided occasionally by Brythunia and Hyperborea, and, secretly, as usual, by Koth. This defeat of the Hyrkanians showed the nations the real power of the western kingdom, whose splendid armies were augmented by mercenaries, many of them recruited among the alien Zingarans, and the barbaric Picts and Shemites. Zamora was reconquered from the Hyrkanians, but the people discovered that they had merely exchanged an eastern master for a western master. Aquilonian soldiers were quartered there, not only to protect the ravaged country, but also to keep the people in subjection. The Hyrkanians were not convinced; three more invasions burst upon the Zamorian borders, and the Lands of Shem, and were hurled back by the Aquilonians, though the Turanian armies grew larger as hordes of steel-clad riders rode out of the east, skirting the southern extremity of the inland sea.

But it was in the west that a power was growing destined to throw down the kings of Aquilonia from their high places. In the north there was incessant bickering along the Cimmerian borders between the black-haired warriors and the Nordheimir; and the Æsir, between wars with the Vanir, assailed Hyperborea and pushed back the frontier, destroying city after city. The Cimmerians also fought the Picts and Bossonians impartially, and several times raided into Aquilonia itself, but their wars were less invasions than mere plundering forays.

But the Picts were growing amazingly in population and power. By a strange twist of fate, it was largely due to the efforts of one man, and he an alien, that they set their feet upon the ways that led to eventual empire. This man was Arus, a Nemedian priest, a natural-born reformer. What turned his mind toward the Picts is not certain, but this much is history—he determined to go into the western wilderness and modify the rude ways of the heathen by the introduction of the gentle worship of Mitra. He was not daunted by the grisly tales of what had happened to traders and explorers before him, and by some whim of fate he came among the people he sought, alone and unarmed, and was not instantly speared.

The Picts had benefited by contact with Hyborian civilization, but they had always fiercely resisted that contact. That is to say, they had learned to work crudely in copper and tin, which were found scantily in their country, and for which latter metal they raided into the mountains of Zingara, or traded hides, whale's teeth, walrus tusks and such few things as savages have to trade. They no longer lived in caves and tree-shelters, but built tents of hides, and crude huts, copied from those of the Bossonians. They still lived mainly by the chase, since their wilds swarmed with game of all sorts, and the rivers and sea with fish, but they had learned how to plant grain, which they did sketchily, preferring to steal it from their neighbors the Bossonians and Zingarans.

They dwelt in clans which were generally at feud with each other, and their simple customs were blood-thirsty and utterly inexplicable to a civilized man, such as Arus of Nemedia. They had no direct contact with the Hyborians, since the Bossonians acted as a buffer between them. But Arus maintained that they were capable of progress, and events proved the truth of his assertion— though scarcely in the way he meant.

Arus was fortunate in being thrown in with a chief of more than usual intelligence—Gorm by name. Gorm cannot be explained, any more than Genghis Khan, Othman, Attila, or any of those individuals, who, born in naked lands among untutored barbarians, yet possess the instinct for conquest and empire-building. In a sort of bastard-Bossonian, the priest made the chief understand his purpose, and though extremely puzzled, Gorm gave him permission to remain among his tribe unbutchered—a case unique in the history of the race. Having learned the language Arus set himself to work to eliminate the more unpleasant phases of Pictish life—such as human sacrifice, blood-feud, and the burning alive of captives. He harangued Gorm at length, whom he found to be an interested, if unresponsive listener. Imagination reconstructs the scene—the black-haired chief, in his tiger-skins and necklace of human teeth, squatting on the dirt floor of the wattle hut, listening intently to the eloquence of the priest, who probably sat on a carven, skin-covered block of mahogany provided in his honor—clad in the silken robes of a Nemedian priest, gesturing with his slender white hands as he expounded the eternal rights and justices which were the truths of Mitra. Doubtless he pointed with repugnance at the rows of skulls which adorned the walls of the hut and urged Gorm to forgive his enemies instead of putting their bleached remnants to such use. Arus was the highest product of an innately artistic race, refined by centuries of civilization; Gorm had behind him a heritage of a hundred thousand years of screaming savagery—the pad of the tiger was in his stealthy step, the grip of the gorilla in his black-nailed hands, the fire that burns in a leopard's eyes burned in his.

Arus was a practical man. He appealed to the savage's sense of material gain; he pointed out the power and splendor of the Hyborian kingdoms, as an example of the power of Mitra, whose teachings and works had lifted them up to their high places. And he spoke of cities, and fertile plains, marble walls and iron chariots, jeweled towers, and horsemen in their glittering armor riding to battle. And Gorm, with the unerring instinct of the barbarian, passed over his words regarding gods and their teachings, and fixed on the material powers thus vividly described. There in that mud-floored wattle hut, with the silk-robed priest on the mahogany block, and the dark-skinned chief crouching in his tiger-hides, was laid the foundations of empire.

As has been said, Arus was a practical man. He dwelt among the Picts and found much that an intelligent man could do to aid humanity, even when that humanity was cloaked in tiger-skins and wore necklaces of human teeth. Like all priests of Mitra, he was instructed in many things. He found that there were vast deposits of iron ore in the Pictish hills, and he taught the natives to mine, smelt and work it into implements— agricultural implements, as he fondly believed. He instituted other reforms, but these were the most important things he did: he instilled in Gorm a desire to see the civilized lands of the world; he taught the Picts how to work in iron; and he established contact between them and the civilized world. At the chiefs request he conducted him and some of his warriors through the Bossonian marches, where the honest villagers stared in amazement, into the glittering outer world.

Arus no doubt thought that he was making converts right and left, because the

Picts listened to him, and refrained from smiting him with their copper axes. But the Pict was little calculated to seriously regard teachings which bade him forgive his enemy and abandon the warpath for the ways of honest drudgery. It has been said that he lacked artistic sense; his whole nature led to war and slaughter. When the priest talked of the glories of the civilized nations, his dark-skinned listeners were intent, not on the ideals of his religion, but on the loot which he unconsciously described in the narration of rich cities and shining lands. When he told how Mitra aided certain kings to overcome their enemies, they paid scant heed to the miracles of Mitra, but they hung on the description of battle-lines, mounted knights, and maneuvers of archers and spearmen. They harkened with keen dark eyes and inscrutable countenances, and they went their ways without comment, and heeded with flattering intentness his instructions as to the working of iron, and kindred arts.

Before his coming they had filched steel weapons and armor from the Bossonians and Zingarans, or had hammered out their own crude arms from copper and bronze. Now a new world opened to them, and the clang of sledges re-echoed throughout the land. And Gorm, by virtue of this new craft, began to assert his dominance over other clans, partly by war, partly by craft and diplomacy, in which latter art he excelled all other barbarians.

Picts now came and went freely into Aquilonia, under safe-conduct, and they returned with more information as to armor-forging and sword-making. More, they entered Aquilonia's mercenary armies, to the unspeakable disgust of the sturdy Bossonians. Aquilonia's kings toyed with the idea of playing the Picts against the Cimmerians, and possibly thus destroying both menaces, but they were too busy with their policies of aggression in the south and east to pay much heed to the vaguely known lands of the west, from which more and more stocky warriors swarmed to take service among the mercenaries.

These warriors, their service completed, went back to their wilderness with good ideas of civilized warfare, and that contempt for civilization which arises from familiarity with it. Drums began to beat in the hills, gathering-fires smoked on the heights, and savage sword-makers hammered their steel on a thousand anvils. By intrigues and forays too numerous and devious to enumerate, Gorm became chief of chiefs, the nearest approach to a king the Picts had had in thousands of years. He had waited long; he was past middle age. But now he moved against the frontiers, not in trade, but in war.

Arus saw his mistake too late; he had not touched the soul of the pagan, in which lurked the hard fierceness of all the ages. His persuasive eloquence had not caused a ripple in the Pictish conscience. Gorm wore a corselet of silvered mail now, instead of the tiger-skin, but underneath he was unchanged—the everlasting barbarian, unmoved by theology or philosophy, his instincts fixed unerringly on rapine and plunder.

The Picts burst on the Bossonian frontiers with fire and sword, not clad in tiger-skins and brandishing copper axes as of yore, but in scale-mail, wielding weapons of keen steel. As for Arus, he was brained by a drunken Pict, while making a last effort to undo the work he had unwittingly done. Gorm was not without gratitude; he caused the skull of the slayer to be set on the top of the priest's cairn. And it is one of the grim ironies of the universe that the stones which covered Arus's body should have been adorned with that last touch of barbarity— above a man to whom violence and blood-vengeance were revolting.

But the newer weapons and mail were not enough to break the lines. For years the superior armaments and sturdy courage of the Bossonians held the invaders at bay, aided, when necessary, by imperial Aquilonian troops. During this time the

Hyrkanians came and went, and Zamora was added to the empire.

Then treachery from an unexpected source broke the Bossonian lines. Before chronicling this treachery, it might be well to glance briefly at the Aquilonian empire. Always a rich kingdom, untold wealth had been rolled in by conquest, and sumptuous splendor had taken the place of simple and hardy living. But degeneracy had not yet sapped the kings and the people; though clad in silks and cloth-of-gold, they were still a vital, virile race. But arrogance was supplanting their former simplicity. They treated less powerful people with growing contempt, levying more and more tributes on the conquered. Argos, Zingara, Ophir, Zamora and the Shemite countries were treated as subjugated provinces, which was especially galling to the proud Zingarans, who often revolted, despite savage retaliations.

Koth was practically tributary, being under Aquilonia's 'protection' against the

Hyrkanians. But Nemedia the western empire had never been able to subdue, although the latter's triumphs were of the defensive sort, and were generally attained with the aid of Hyperborean armies. During this period Aquilonia's only defeats were: her failure to annex Nemedia; the rout of an army sent into Cimmeria; and the almost complete destruction of an army by the Æsir. Just as the Hyrkanians found themselves unable to withstand the heavy cavalry charges of the Aquilonians, so the latter, invading the snow-countries, were overwhelmed by the ferocious hand-to-hand fighting of the Nordics. But Aquilonia's conquests were pushed to the Nilus, where a Stygian army was defeated with great slaughter, and the king of Stygia sent tribute—once at least—to divert invasion of his kingdom. Brythunia was reduced in a series of whirlwind wars, and preparations were made to subjugate the ancient rival at last—Nemedia.

With their glittering hosts greatly increased by mercenaries, the Aquilonians moved against their old-time foe, and it seemed as if the thrust were destined to crush the last shadow of Nemedian independence. But contentions arose between the Aquilonians and their Bossonian auxiliaries.

As the inevitable result of imperial expansion, the Aquilonians had become haughty and intolerant. They derided the ruder, unsophisticated Bossonians, and hard feeling grew between them—the Aquilonians despising the Bossonians and the latter resenting the attitude of their masters—who now boldly called themselves such, and treated the Bossonians like conquered subjects, taxing them exorbitantly, and conscripting them for their wars of territorial expansion—wars the profits of which the Bossonians shared little. Scarcely enough men were left in the marches to guard the frontier, and hearing of Pictish outrages in their homelands, whole

Bossonian regiments quit the Nemedian campaign and marched to the western frontier, where they defeated the dark-skinned invaders in a great battle.

This desertion, however, was the direct cause of Aquilonia's defeat by the desperate Nemedians, and brought down on the Bossonians the cruel wrath of the imperialists—intolerant and short-sighted as imperialists invariably are. Aquilonian regiments were secretly brought to the borders of the marches, the Bossonian chiefs were invited to attend a great conclave, and, in the guise of an expedition against the Picts, bands of savage Shemitish soldiers were quartered among the unsuspecting villagers. The unarmed chiefs were massacred, the Shemites turned on their stunned hosts with torch and sword, and the armored imperial hosts were hurled ruthlessly on the unsuspecting people. From north to south the marches were ravaged and the Aquilonian armies marched back from the borders, leaving a ruined and devastated land behind them.

And then the Pictish invasion burst in full power along those borders. It was no mere raid, but the concerted rush of a whole nation, led by chiefs who had served in Aquilonian armies, and planned and directed by Gorm—an old man now, but with the fire of his fierce ambition undimmed. This time there were no strong walled villages in their path, manned by sturdy archers, to hold back the rush until the imperial troops could be brought up. The remnants of the Bossonians were swept out of existence, and the blood-mad barbarians swarmed into Aquilonia, looting and burning, before the legions, warring again with the Nemedians, could be marched into the west. Zingara seized this opportunity to throw off the yoke, which example was followed by Corinthia and the Shemites. Whole regiments of mercenaries and vassals mutinied and marched back to their own countries, looting and burning as they went. The Picts surged irresistibly eastward, and host after host was trampled beneath their feet. Without their Bossonian archers the Aquilonians found themselves unable to cope with the terrible arrow-fire of the barbarians. From all parts of the empire legions were recalled to resist the onrush, while from the wilderness horde after horde swarmed forth, in apparently inexhaustible supply. And in the midst of this chaos, the Cimmerians swept down from their hills, completing the ruin. They looted cities, devastated the country, and retired into the hills with their plunder, but the Picts occupied the land they had over-run. And the Aquilonian empire went down in fire and blood.

Then again the Hyrkanians rode from the blue east. The withdrawal of the imperial legions from Zamora was their incitement. Zamora fell easy prey to their thrusts, and the Hyrkanian king established his capital in the largest city of the country. This invasion was from the ancient Hyrkanian kingdom of Turan, on the shores of the inland sea, but another, more savage Hyrkanian thrust came from the north. Hosts of steel-clad riders galloped around the northern extremity of the inland sea, traversed the icy deserts, entered the steppes, driving the aborigines before them, and launched themselves against the western kingdoms. These newcomers were not at first allies with the Turanians, but skirmished with them as with the Hyborians; new drifts of eastern warriors bickered and fought, until all were united under a great chief, who came riding from the very shores of the eastern ocean. With no Aquilonian armies to oppose them, they were invincible. They swept over and subjugated Brythunia, and devastated southern Hyperborea, and Corinthia. They swept into the Cimmerian hills, driving the black-haired barbarians before them, but among the hills, where cavalry was less effectual, the Cimmerians turned on them, and only a disorderly retreat, at the end of a whole day of bloody fighting, saved the

Hyrkanian hosts from complete annihilation.

While these events had been transpiring, the kingdoms of Shem had conquered their ancient master, Koth, and had been defeated in an attempted invasion of Stygia. But scarcely had they completed their degradation of Koth, when they were over-run by the Hyrkanians, and found themselves subjugated by sterner masters than the Hyborians had ever been. Meanwhile the Picts had made themselves complete masters of Aquilonia, practically blotting out the inhabitants. They had broken over the borders of Zingara, and thousands of Zingarans, fleeing the slaughter into Argos, threw themselves on the mercy of the westward-sweeping Hyrkanians, who settled them in Zamora as subjects. Behind them as they fled, Argos was enveloped in the flame and slaughter of Pictish conquest, and the slayers swept into Ophir and clashed with the westward-riding Hyrkanians. The latter, after their conquest of Shem, had overthrown a Stygian army at the Nilus and over-run the country as far south as the black kingdom of Amazon, of whose people they brought back thousands as captives, settling them among the Shemites. Possibly they would have completed their conquests in Stygia, adding it to their widening empire, but for the fierce thrusts of the Picts against their western conquests.

Nemedia, unconquerable by Hyborians, reeled between the riders of the east and the swordsmen of the west, when a tribe of Æsir, wandering down from their snowy lands, came into the kingdom, and were engaged as mercenaries; they proved such able warriors that they not only beat off the Hyrkanians, but halted the eastward advance of the Picts.

The world at that time presents some such picture: a vast Pictish empire, wild, rude and barbaric, stretches from the coasts of Vanaheim in the north to the southern-most shores of Zingara. It stretches east to include all Aquilonia except Gunderland, the northern-most province, which, as a separate kingdom in the hills, survived the fall of the empire, and still maintains its independence. The Pictish empire also includes Argos, Ophir, the western part of Koth, and the western-most lands of Shem. Opposed to this barbaric empire is the empire of the Hyrkanians, of which the northern boundaries are the ravaged lines of Hyperborea, and the southern, the deserts south of the lands of Shem. Zamora, Brythunia, the Border Kingdom, Corinthia, most of Koth, and all the eastern lands of Shem are included in this empire. The borders of Cimmeria are intact; neither Pict nor Hyrkanian has been able to subdue these warlike barbarians. Nemedia, dominated by the Æsir mercenaries, resists all invasions. In the north Nordheim, Cimmeria and Nemedia separate the conquering races, but in the south, Koth has become a battle-ground where Picts and Hyrkanians war incessantly. Sometimes the eastern warriors expel the barbarians from the kingdom entirely; again the plains and cities are in the hands of the western invaders. In the far south, Stygia, shaken by the Hyrkanian invasion, is being encroached upon by the great black kingdoms. And in the far north, the Nordic tribes are restless, warring continually with the Cimmerians, and sweeping the Hyperborean frontiers.

Gorm was slain by Hialmar, a chief of the Nemedian Æsir. He was a very old man, nearly a hundred years old. In the seventy-five years which had elapsed since he first heard the tale of empires from the lips of Arus—a long time in the life of a man, but a brief space in the tale of nations—he had welded an empire from straying savage clans, he had overthrown a civilization. He who had been born in a mud-walled, wattle-roofed hut, in his old age sat on golden thrones, and gnawed joints of beef presented to him on golden dishes by naked slave-girls who were the daughters of kings. Conquest and the acquiring of wealth altered not the Pict; out of the ruins of the crushed civilization no new culture arose phoenix-like. The dark hands which shattered the artistic glories of the conquered never tried to copy them. Though he sat among the glittering ruins of shattered palaces and clad his hard body in the silks of vanquished kings, the Pict remained the eternal barbarian, ferocious, elemental, interested only in the naked primal principles of life, unchanging, unerring in his instincts which were all for war and plunder, and in which arts and the cultured progress of humanity had no place. Not so with the Æsir who settled in Nemedia. These soon adopted many of the ways of their civilized allies, modified powerfully, however, by their own intensely virile and alien culture.

For a short age Pict and Hyrkanian snarled at each other over the ruins of the world they had conquered. Then began the glacier ages, and the great Nordic drift. Before the southward moving ice-fields the northern tribes drifted, driving kindred clans before them. The Æsir blotted out the ancient kingdom of Hyperborea, and across its ruins came to grips with the Hyrkanians. Nemedia had already become a Nordic kingdom, ruled by the descendants of the Æsir mercenaries. Driven before the onrushing tides of Nordic invasion, the Cimmerians were on the march, and neither army nor city stood before them. They surged across and completely destroyed the kingdom of Gunderland, and marched across ancient Aquilonia, hewing their irresistible way through the Pictish hosts. They defeated the Nordic-Nemedians and sacked some of their cities, but did not halt. They continued eastward, overthrowing a Hyrkanian army on the borders of Brythunia.

Behind them hordes of Æsir and Vanir swarmed into the lands, and the Pictish empire reeled beneath their strokes. Nemedia was overthrown, and the half-civilized Nordics fled before their wilder kinsmen, leaving the cities of Nemedia ruined and deserted. These fleeing Nordics, who had adopted the name of the older kingdom, and to whom the term Nemedian henceforth refers, came into the ancient land of Koth, expelled both Picts and Hyrkanians, and aided the people of Shem to throw off the Hyrkanian yoke. All over the western world, the Picts and Hyrkanians were staggering before this younger, fiercer people. A band of Æsir drove the eastern riders from Brythunia and settled there themselves, adopting the name for themselves. The Nordics who had conquered Hyperborea assailed their eastern enemies so savagely that the dark-skinned descendants of the Lemurians retreated into the steppes, pushed irresistibly back toward Vilayet.

Meanwhile the Cimmerians, wandering southeastward, destroyed the ancient Hyrkanian kingdom of Turan, and settled on the southwestern shores of the inland sea. The power of the eastern conquerors was broken. Before the attacks of the Nordheimir and the Cimmerians, they destroyed all their cities, butchered such captives as were not fit to make the long march, and then, herding thousands of slaves before them, rode back into the mysterious east, skirting the northern edge of the sea, and vanishing from western history, until they rode out of the east again, thousands of years later, as Huns, Mongols, Tatars and Turks. With them in their retreat went thousands of Zamorians and Zingarans, who were settled together far to the east, formed a mixed race, and emerged ages afterward as gypsies.

Meanwhile, also, a tribe of Vanir adventurers had passed along the Pictish coast southward, ravaged ancient Zingara, and come into Stygia, which, oppressed by a cruel aristocratic ruling class, was staggering under the thrusts of the black kingdoms to the south. The red-haired Vanir led the slaves in a general revolt, overthrew the reigning class, and set themselves up as a caste of conquerors. They subjugated the northern-most black kingdoms, and built a vast southern empire, which they called

Egypt. From these red-haired conquerors the earlier Pharaohs boasted descent.

The western world was now dominated by Nordic barbarians. The Picts still held Aquilonia and part of Zingara, and the western coast of the continent. But east to Vilayet, and from the Arctic circle to the lands of Shem, the only inhabitants were roving tribes of Nordheimir, excepting the Cimmerians, settled in the old Turanian kingdom. There were no cities anywhere, except in Stygia and the lands of Shem; the invading tides of Picts, Hyrkanians, Cimmerians and Nordics had levelled them in ruins, and the once dominant Hyborians had vanished from the earth, leaving scarcely a trace of their blood in the veins of their conquerors. Only a few names of lands, tribes and cities remained in the languages of the barbarians, to come down through the centuries connected with distorted legend and fable, until the whole history of the Hyborian age was lost sight of in a cloud of myths and fantasies. Thus in the speech of the gypsies lingered the terms Zingara and Zamora; the Æsir who dominated Nemedia were called Nemedians, and later figured in Irish history, and the Nordics who settled in Brythunia were known as Brythunians, Brythons or Britons.

There was no such thing, at that time, as a consolidated Nordic empire. As always, the tribes had each its own chief or king, and they fought savagely among themselves. What their destiny might have been will not be known, because another terrific convulsion of the earth, carving out the lands as they are known to moderns, hurled all into chaos again. Great strips of the western coast sank; Vanaheim and western Asgard—uninhabited and glacier-haunted wastes for a hundred years—vanished beneath the waves. The ocean flowed around the mountains of western Cimmeria to form the North Sea; these mountains became the islands later known as England, Scotland and Ireland, and the waves rolled over what had been the Pictish wilderness and the Bossonian marches. In the north the Baltic Sea was formed, cutting Asgard into the peninsulas later known as Norway, Sweden and Denmark, and far to the south the Stygian continent was broken away from the rest of the world, on the line of cleavage formed by the river Nilus in its westward trend. Over Argos, western Koth and the western lands of Shem, washed the blue ocean men later called the Mediterranean. But where land sank elsewhere, a vast expanse west of Stygia rose out of the waves, forming the whole western half of the continent of Africa.

The buckling of the land thrust up great mountain ranges in the central part of the northern continent. Whole Nordic tribes were blotted out, and the rest retreated eastward. The territory about the slowly drying inland sea was not affected, and there, on the western shores, the Nordic tribes began a pastoral existence, living in more or less peace with the Cimmerians, and gradually mixing with them. In the west the remnants of the Picts, reduced by the cataclysm once more to the status of stone-age savages, began, with the incredible virility of their race, once more to possess the land, until, at a later age, they were overthrown by the westward drift of the Cimmerians and Nordics. This was so long after the breaking-up of the continent that only meaningless legends told of former empires.

This drift comes within the reach of modern history and need not be repeated. It resulted from a growing population which thronged the steppes west of the inland sea—which still later, much reduced in size, was known as the Caspian—to such an extent that migration became an economic necessity. The tribes moved southward, northward and westward, into those lands now known as India, Asia Minor and central and western Europe.

They came into these countries as Aryans. But there were variations among these primitive Aryans, some of which are still recognized today, others which have long been forgotten. The blond Achaians, Gauls and Britons, for instance, were descendants of pure-blooded Æsir. The Nemedians of Irish legendry were the Nemedian Æsir. The Danes were descendants of pure-blooded Vanir; the Goths—ancestors of the other Scandinavian and Germanic tribes, including the Anglo-Saxons—were descendants of a mixed race whose elements contained Vanir, Æsir and Cimmerian strains. The Gaels, ancestors of the Irish and Highland Scotch, descended from pure-blooded Cimmerian clans. The Cymric tribes of Britain were a mixed Nordic-Cimmerian race which preceded the purely Nordic Britons into the isles, and thus gave rise to a legend of Gaelic priority. The Cimbri who fought Rome were of the same blood, as well as the Gimmerai of the Assyrians and Grecians, and Gomer of the Hebrews. Other clans of the Cimmerians adventured east of the drying inland sea, and a few centuries later mixed with Hyrkanian blood, returned westward as Scythians. The original ancestors of the Gaels gave their name to modern Crimea.

The ancient Sumerians had no connection with the western race. They were a mixed people, of Hyrkanian and Shemitish bloods, who were not taken with the conquerors in their retreat. Many tribes of Shem escaped that captivity, and from pure-blooded Shemites, or Shemites mixed with Hyborian or Nordic blood, were descended the Arabs, Israelites, and other straighter-featured Semites. The Canaanites, or Alpine Semites, traced their descent from Shemitish ancestors mixed with the Kushites settled among them by their Hyrkanian masters; the Elamites were a typical race of this type. The short, thick-limbed Etruscans, base of the Roman race, were descendants of a people of mixed Stygian, Hyrkanian and Pictish strains, and originally lived in the ancient kingdom of Koth. The Hyrkanians, retreating to the eastern shores of the continent, evolved into the tribes later known as Tatars, Huns, Mongols and Turks.

The origins of other races of the modern world may be similarly traced; in almost every case, older far than they realize, their history stretches back into the mists of the forgotten Hyborian age....

Printed in Great Britain
by Amazon

45170396R00037